big NATE

ALOHA!

Complete Your *Big Nate* Collection

big NATE
ALOHA!

by LINCOLN PEIRCE

TODAY, CLASS, YOU'LL BEGIN A PAINTING FROM **OBSERVATION**!

YOU CAN SET UP A STILL LIFE, PAINT WHAT YOU SEE OUT THE WINDOW, DO A SELF-PORTRAIT...
CAN I PAINT AN ANIMAL?

AN ANIMAL?... WELL, LET'S SEE. THERE **ARE** A FEW CRITTERS IN THE BUILDING...

THERE'S A FISH TANK IN THE TEACHER'S LOUNGE...
MR. GALVIN KEEPS A TURTLE IN HIS LAB...

...AND OF COURSE, YOU'VE SEEN THE GERBIL IN MRS. GODFREY'S ROOM!
DO ANY OF THOSE INTEREST YOU?

I WAS... UH... THINKING OF SOMETHING A BIT MORE... Y'KNOW... **CANINE**.

NATE, THE SCHOOL IS NOT GOING TO BUY A **DOG** FOR YOU TO PAINT.

NO OFFENSE, SHERMAN, BUT YOU WEREN'T MY FIRST CHOICE.
THAT'S THE STORY OF MY LIFE.

HEH HEH!
WHAT'S SO FUNNY?

LOOK OVER THERE!

CHECK OUT THE **LAWN GNOME**!
HA HA!

THAT'S A RIOT!
HE LOOKS LIKE HE'S FLOATING IN THE OCEAN!
HA HA
HA HA
HA HA
HA HA

HA HA HA HA HA
HA HA HA HA HA

HA HA HA... HEH...
SKRATCH SKRATCH
SKRATCH SKRATCH
SKRATCH

HOW QUICKLY LIFE CAN TAKE A SINISTER TURN.
BUT HEY, HE'S STILL SMILING!
Peirce

I NEED TO FIND OUT IF DAISY LIKES ME.
WHY?

BECAUSE, FRANCIS! WOULDN'T YOU WANT TO KNOW IF A GIRL LIKED YOU?
WELL, DO YOU LIKE HER?

OF COURSE I LIKE HER! I GAVE HER A VALENTINE, DIDN'T I?
WHAT DO YOU LIKE ABOUT HER?

THAT SHE MIGHT POSSIBLY LIKE ME.
SOUNDS LIKE DESTINY.
Peirce

FRANCIS, HOW ABOUT TRYING TO FIND OUT IF DAISY LIKES ME?
NO WAY. LEAVE ME OUT OF IT.

I DON'T LIKE PRETENDING TO HAVE A NORMAL CONVERSATION WITH SOMEONE WHEN WHAT I'M **REALLY** DOING IS PUMPING THEM FOR INFORMATION!

I'M LOUSY AT THAT. YOU NEED TO FIND SOMEONE WHO'S A BETTER ACTOR THAN I AM.

AHEM!
BUT I DON'T **KNOW** ANY GOOD ACTORS!

DEE DEE! MAYBE **YOU** CAN FIND OUT IF DAISY LIKES ME!
OF **COURSE** I CAN!

BUT DON'T BE **OBVIOUS** ABOUT IT!
ME? **NEVER!**

I'M AN ACCOMPLISHED ACTRESS, MY FRIEND! I SPECIALIZE IN ROLES OF **DEPTH** AND **SUBTLETY!**

...OR HAVE YOU FORGOTTEN MY PERFORMANCE AS HYENA #2 IN THE DRAMA CLUB'S PRODUCTION OF "THE LION KING"?
I DON'T THINK ANYONE HAS.
Peirce

SO WHAT'S YOUR STRATEGY? HOW WILL YOU FIND OUT IF DAISY LIKES ME?
I'M JUST GOING TO GET HER TALKING, THAT'S ALL!

TALKING ABOUT WHAT?
ABOUT **STUFF**.
WHAT KIND OF STUFF?
I DON'T **KNOW** YET.
ABOUT **ME?**
MAYBE.

OKAY, BUT WHAT WILL YOU-?
NATE, STOP **HOUNDING** ME! I'LL DO YOUR LITTLE ERRAND! **RELAX!**

DON'T MAKE ME SOUND DESPERATE!
Peirce

HI, DAISY! ANYONE SITTING HERE?
NOPE!

SO! *AHEM!* WHAT DID YOU THINK OF THAT MATH–
THIS IS ABOUT NATE, RIGHT?

NATE? UM, I DON'T KNOW WHAT YOU–
YOU CAN **PRETEND** WE'RE JUST CHATTING, DEE DEE, BUT I CAN SEE RIGHT THROUGH YOU!

YOU'RE NOT THAT GOOD AN ACTRESS!
HA HA! OKAY, YOU'RE— WAIT, I'M WHAT?
Peirce

SO I'M GUESSING NATE WANTS TO KNOW IF I LIKE HIM.
WELL, DO YOU?

I'M NOT REALLY SURE. I DON'T KNOW HIM THAT WELL. I MEAN, HE SEEMS FUN. AND HE'S KIND OF CUTE.

BUT HE ALSO ACTS LIKE KIND OF AN IDIOT SOMETIMES.
SNORT! **SOME-**TIMES?

NOW THEY'RE BOTH LAUGHING.
COULD BE GOOD. COULD BE BAD.
Peirce

WELL? **WELL**?
WELL WHAT?

DID YOU TALK TO DAISY?
OH. YES. YES, I DID.

AND?
A GOOD ACTRESS KNOWS HOW TO BUILD SUSPENSE.
Peirce

SPILL IT, DEE DEE! DID YOU ASK DAISY IF SHE LIKES ME?
YES, I DID.

AND DID SHE GIVE YOU AN ANSWER?
YES, SHE DID.

WELL, WHAT WAS IT?
SHE HAS NO IDEA.

ARRGH!
THIS IS FUN!
Peirce

HOW COME DAISY'S NOT SURE IF SHE LIKES ME?
BECAUSE SHE DOESN'T **KNOW** YOU WELL ENOUGH!

AND BY THE **WAY**, NATE: **YOU** DON'T KNOW **HER**, EITHER!
WHAT? OF **COURSE** I KNOW HER!

OH, YOU **DO**? THEN WHAT COLOR ARE HER EYES?
UH... HAZEL.

"HAZEL" IS WHAT PEOPLE SAY WHEN THEY DON'T KNOW THE COLOR OF SOMEONE'S EYES.
BUSTED.
Peirce

ALL DAISY'S SAYING, NATE, IS THAT THE TWO OF YOU SHOULD GET TO KNOW EACH OTHER BETTER!

THEN YOU CAN DECIDE IF YOU LIKE ONE ANOTHER!
BUT I ALREADY **KNOW** I LIKE DAISY!

I GAVE HER A **VALENTINE**, DIDN'T I?

THIS IS WHEN I REMIND YOU THAT YOU GAVE **EVERYONE** A VALENTINE.
NOT EVERYONE! NOT GINA, MRS. GODFREY, OR THAT LUNCH LADY WITH THE NOSE RING!
Peirce

WHAT'S THIS?
HEY, **YOU'RE** THE ONE WHO SAID DAISY AND I NEED TO GET TO KNOW EACH OTHER!

SO I'M MAKING A LIST OF FUN FACTS ABOUT MYSELF: MY HOBBIES, MY FAVORITE MOVIES, STUFF LIKE THAT!

I'LL GIVE THIS TO HER ON OUR FIRST DATE!
WHY NOT GET ACQUAINTED BY JUST **TALKING**?

DUH. BECAUSE WE'LL BE TOO BUSY MAKING OUT.
UH-HUH.
Peirce

THERE'S DAISY! I'M GONNA GO TALK TO HER!
REMEMBER TO BE YOURSELF, NATE!

DON'T TRY BEING MR. SMOOTH AND ACTING ALL CHEESY!
CHEESY? **ME**?

I DON'T HAVE A CHEESY BONE IN MY BODY! I'M JUST GOING TO WALK UP TO HER AND SAY...

ALOHA.
Peirce

SO! DAISY! DEE DEE TELLS ME YOU THINK WE SHOULD GET TO KNOW EACH OTHER BETTER!
UH-HUH!

WE CAN HANG OUT A LITTLE BIT... MAYBE GO ON A FEW DATES...

...AND THEN, AFTER A COUPLE MONTHS, WE CAN DECIDE IF WE LIKE EACH OTHER!
MONTHS?

I MEAN, THERE'S NO RUSH, RIGHT?
RIGHT, RIGHT. MONTHS?
peirce

YOU THINK IT'LL TAKE **MONTHS** 'TIL WE KNOW IF WE LIKE EACH OTHER?
WELL... MAYBE NOT MONTHS.

BUT IT **DOES** TAKE TIME TO GET TO KNOW SOMEONE.
NOT TRUE, DAISY! LISTEN!

I LIKE COMICS, DOGS, SPORTS, CHEEZ DOODLES, AND "STAR TREK: THE NEXT GENERATION." I HATE CATS, EGG SALAD, FIGURE SKATING, MRS. GODFREY, AND FORTUNE COOKIES THAT AREN'T REALLY FORTUNES.

SHOULD I BE TAKING NOTES?
OKAY, NOW **YOU** GO!

WE CAN'T GET TO KNOW EACH OTHER ALL AT **ONCE**, NATE! LET'S JUST LET IT HAPPEN NATURALLY!

JUST BY HAVING CASUAL CONVERSATIONS, WE'LL START TO GRADUALLY LEARN STUFF ABOUT ONE ANOTHER!
GOT IT!

YOU GONNA FINISH THOSE CHIPS?
IT'S A START.
Peirce

WHY DON'T WE TALK ABOUT HOW OUR DAY IS GOING SO FAR?
OKAY. I'LL GO FIRST.

FIRST PERIOD I HAD SOCIAL STUDIES, AND MRS. GODFREY SCREAMED AT ME FOR MAKING TOO MUCH NOISE DURING RICKY LAMBERT'S REPORT ON CALVIN COOLIDGE.

SECOND PERIOD I HAD ENGLISH, AND MS. CLARKE SCREAMED AT ME BECAUSE MY HOME-WORK HAD PIZZA STAINS ALL OVER IT.

THIRD PERIOD I HAD MATH, AND MR. STAPLES SCREAMED AT ME BECAUSE—
I'M SENSING A THEME.
Peirce

AH, HERE'S WHAT I LIKE TO SEE: P.S. 38's HOTTEST NEW POTENTIAL COUPLE HANGING OUT IN THE LIBRARY!

HEY, YOU KNOW WHAT WOULD MAKE THIS LITTLE SCENE EVEN MORE ROMANTIC? SOME MUSIC!
AHEM!

OHHHHH SOME ENCHANTED EVENING...
Peirce

OUT.
LET'S HEAR IT FOR LIBRARIANS.

HOW'S IT GOING WITH DAISY?
GOOD! WE'RE GOING TO A MOVIE THIS WEEKEND!

YEAH? WHICH ONE?
I DON'T EVEN CARE. I'M JUST TRYING TO FIND OUT HOW DAISY LIKES HER POPCORN.

IT'S A PROVEN FACT THAT YOU CAN TELL A LOT ABOUT SOME-ONE BASED ON HOW THEY LIKE THEIR POPCORN!

I GO NO BUTTER, LIGHT SALT.
I GO LIGHT BUTTER, HEAVY SALT.
I GO HEAVY BUTTER, GARLIC SALT, AND THEN I SPRINKLE IT WITH SNO-CAPS!
Peirce

HI, DAISY! READY FOR THE MOVIE?
YUP! LET'S GO!

BY THE WAY, I ASKED JENNY AND ARTUR IF THEY WANTED TO MEET US THERE.
OH. YOU DID?

YEAH, BUT THEY'RE BUSY DOING SOMETHING ELSE.

SO IT'S JUST THE TWO OF US!
ROWR!

WOW! BIG CROWD!
NATE... UM... ABOUT THE MOVIE...

I KNOW WE AGREED TO SEE "KONG: SKULL ISLAND." BUT WOULD YOU MIND IF WE SAW SOMETHING DIFFERENT?
NOT AT ALL! NO PROBLEM!

I DON'T CARE **WHAT** WE SEE!
GOOD, 'CAUSE I WANT TO WATCH "BEFORE I FALL."

I CARE WHAT WE SEE.
I **LOVE** A GOOD CHICK FLICK!

WANNA GET A SNACK?
SURE! I'LL HAVE SOME JUNIOR MINTS!

A BOX OF JUNIOR MINTS AND A BAG OF CHEEZ DOODLES, PLEASE.
OOH. CHEEZ DOODLES?

I CAN'T EAT THOSE. THEY'RE TOO INTENSE FOR ME.

I SENSE A GREAT DISTURBANCE IN THE FORCE.
Peirce

I THINK DAISY WANTS TO HOLD HANDS.
I THINK NATE WANTS TO HOLD HANDS.

AHEM! WANNA HOLD HANDS?
UM... OKAY.

TOO CLAMMY.
TOO SWEATY.

IT SEEMED LIKE YOU DIDN'T REALLY LIKE THE MOVIE.
WHAT?

ARE YOU KIDDING? OF **COURSE** I LIKED THE MOVIE! I **LOVED** THE MOVIE! IT WAS GOOD! IT WAS **GREAT**!

UH-HUH...

YOU WERE SNORING.
OH, WAS I?

I THINK DAISY WANTS ME TO KISS HER GOOD-NIGHT.
I THINK NATE'S GOING TO KISS ME GOOD-NIGHT.

WELL... G'NIGHT.
G'NIGHT.

SMACK!

ZILCH.
NOTHIN'.
Peirce

HOW WAS YOUR HOT DATE WITH DAISY?
NOT VERY HOT.

WHAT? YOU DIDN'T GET ALONG?
WE GOT ALONG FINE, BUT... THERE WAS NO SPARK! NO CHEMISTRY!

BUMMER.
YEAH, BUT HERE'S THE AWKWARD PART...

SHE'S OBVIOUSLY **CRAZY** ABOUT ME!
HE'S OBVIOUSLY **CRAZY** ABOUT ME!
Peirce

SO THE ROMANCE WITH DAISY IS GOING NOWHERE?
YOU CAN SAY THAT AGAIN.

BUT HOW DO I TELL **HER** THAT? SHE'S **NUTS** ABOUT ME!

LOOK, THERE SHE IS — OBVIOUSLY TELLING HER FRIENDS ALL ABOUT OUR DATE.

...CHEEZ DOODLE BREATH.
REALLY?
EW.

IS IT TRUE YOU AND DAISY AREN'T GONNA BE A COUPLE?
LOOKS THAT WAY.

AW. YOU GUYS WOULD HAVE BEEN CUTE TOGETHER.
THAT'S WHAT I THOUGHT. BUT THERE'S NO TINGLE, KNOW WHAT I MEAN?

WHEN YOU REALLY LIKE SOMEBODY, YOU'RE SUPPOSED TO GET THAT TINGLY FEELING ALL OVER!

I GOT TINGLY DURING MATH YESTERDAY, BUT ONLY BECAUSE MY BUTT FELL ASLEEP.
THANKS, CHAD. VERY HELPFUL.
Peirce

IT'S GOT TO BE DONE.
WHAT'S GOT TO BE DONE?

I'VE GOT TO TELL DAISY IT WON'T WORK OUT BETWEEN US! AND SHE'S GOING TO BE HEARTBROKEN!

WELL... GOOD LUCK, DUDE.
WAIT, WAIT. DO YOU HAVE ANY FOOD?

DO I HAVE ANY **FOOD**?
I CAN'T SHATTER HER WORLD ON AN EMPTY STOMACH.
BEEYOWWL
Peirce

UH... HI, DAISY... CAN I TALK TO YOU?
HI, NATE. I WANT TO TALK TO YOU, TOO.

I DON'T THINK WE SHOULD GO ON ANY MORE DATES, NATE.
WHA-? HEY, THAT'S WHAT **I** WAS GOING TO SAY!

THE OTHER NIGHT, I WAS SORT OF-
AWKWARD? BOY, WERE YOU **EVER**.
NO, I MEAN I DIDN'T FEEL-
NEITHER DID **I**! I FELT **NOTHING**!

THIS IS GOING SO WELL.
WHEN YOU KISSED ME, I WENT **DEAD** INSIDE!
Peirce

HOW'D IT GO WITH DAISY? DID YOU LET HER DOWN EASY?
HUH?...OH! YEAH!

SHE WAS...UM... PRETTY UPSET, BUT... *KOFF!*... LIKE YOU SAID, I LET HER DOWN EASY!

HEY, NATE! I HEAR DAISY DUMPED YOU!

OOH! ALTER-NATIVE FACTS!
IS IT TRUE YOU KISS LIKE A DAMP DISHRAG?

NO! NO! NO!

YOU'RE SUPPOSED TO ATTACK THE BALL, NOT LET IT ATTACK YOU!

BUT IT MIGHT HIT ME IN THE FACE!
UNACCEPTABLE, RED! YOU! TAKE OVER AT SHORTSTOP!
ME?

BUT I'M AN OUTFIELDER!
NOT TODAY, SONNY! TODAY YOU'RE A SHORTSTOP!

EMBRACE IT, KID! THIS IS YOUR CHANCE TO SHINE!

SO GO AHEAD! SHINE!
KRAK!

LATER...
THAT'S SOME SHINER!

THE TEST

QUESTION 1:
HOW EASY IS THIS?

QUESTION 2:
SHOULD I COME BACK TO THIS ONE?

QUESTION 3:
WHY CAN'T I THINK?

QUESTION 4:
AM I SUPPOSED TO KNOW THIS?

QUESTION 5:
WHAT THE-?

QUESTION 6:
WHO CARES?
QUESTION 7:
IS THIS A JOKE?

QUESTION 8:
DOES IT REALLY MATTER?

BONUS QUESTION:
CAN I GO TO THE NURSE'S OFFICE?
Peirce

I'M GLAD BASEBALL'S STARTING, COACH. IT'LL HELP ME GET OVER MY RELATIONSHIP PROBLEMS.
OACH

RELATIONSHIP PROBLEMS?
YEAH. WANNA HEAR WHAT HAPPENED?
COACH

I STEPPED UP TO THE PLATE, AND SHE THREW ME A CURVEBALL. I SWUNG FOR THE FENCES, AND SHE ROBBED ME OF A HOME RUN.

IN THE BOTTOM OF THE NINTH, OR...?
TOP OF THE FIRST.
Peirce

IS CRESSLY'S BAKERY SPONSORING US AGAIN THIS YEAR, COACH?
YUP! WE'RE STILL THE CUPCAKES!

AARRGH! CUPCAKES IS SUCH A STUPID NAME!

CAN'T WE NAME OURSELVES SOMETHING **ELSE**?
HOW ABOUT THE STICKY BUNS?

CHAD, I'M NOT PLAYING FOR A TEAM CALLED THE STICKY BUNS.
OR MAYBE THE WHOOPIE PIES! THAT SOUNDS SO CHEERY!

CHESTER! YOU'RE BACK ON OUR TEAM THIS YEAR?
YEAH

I DIDN'T LIKE PLAYING FOR "AL'S AUTO GLASS."
AH-HA! I KNEW IT!

I SAID: "I'LL BET CHESTER MISSES US," AND YOU DID! YOU MISSED US! RIGHT, CHESTER?

STOP TALKING OR I'LL RIP YOUR LIPS OFF.
HEAR THAT, GUYS? IT'S JUST LIKE OLD TIMES!
Peirce

NOW THAT CHESTER'S BACK ON THE TEAM, THERE WILL BE THE INEVITABLE LOVE TRIANGLE.
WHAT?

HE AND I ARE IN LOVE, BUT YOU'RE IN LOVE WITH ME TOO, SO...
KIM, I'M **NOT** IN LOVE WITH YOU!

TRY NOT TO BE OBVIOUS ABOUT IT. OTHERWISE, HE'LL FLY INTO A JEALOUS RAGE.
I'M NOT BEING OBVIOUS ABOUT ANYTHING!

STOMP! STOMP! STOMP!
OOP. TOO LATE.
Peirce

I KNOW IT'S A LITTLE CHILLY OUT HERE, GANG, BUT IT'S GOING TO BE **WORTH** IT!

ONCE THE SEASON STARTS, WE'LL BE **WAY** AHEAD OF THE OTHER TEAMS! YOU KNOW WHY?

BECAUSE WHILE **WE'RE** OUT HERE PRACTICING, **THEY'RE** SITTING AROUND EATING **JUNK FOOD** AND PLAYING **VIDEO GAMES**!
COACH

AFTER THIS, WANNA GO TO MY HOUSE TO EAT JUNK FOOD AND PLAY VIDEO GAMES?
ABSOLUTELY.
Peirce

THINK I'LL GET A CHANCE TO PITCH THIS YEAR, COACH?
UH... WE'LL SEE.

HEY, **HERE'S** AN IDEA! I'LL THROW SOME BATTING PRACTICE, AND IF I DO OKAY, MAYBE I CAN PITCH IN A REAL GAME!

CLONK!
OW!

SORRY, CHAD.
THE SAD PART IS, CHAD WAS STANDING IN THE ON-DECK CIRCLE.
ACH
Peirce

COACH, HOW COME WE HAVE TO PUT UP WITH **COACH JOHN** AGAIN THIS YEAR?
CO

THE GUY IS A **PSYCHO**!

HE'S ALWAYS **YELLING**! HE'S WAY TOO **INTENSE**! HE PUTS ALL THIS **PRESSURE** ON US! I MEAN, PUMP THE **BRAKES**, DUDE!
CH

WELL, I NEED AN ASSISTANT COACH, NATE. WHAT DO YOU SUGGEST?

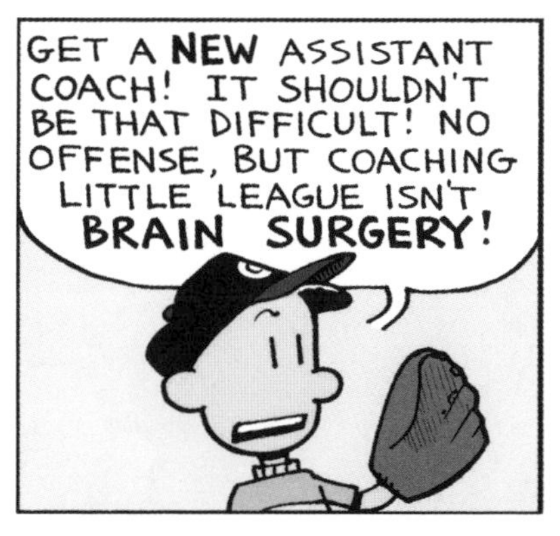
GET A **NEW** ASSISTANT COACH! IT SHOULDN'T BE THAT DIFFICULT! NO OFFENSE, BUT COACHING LITTLE LEAGUE ISN'T **BRAIN SURGERY**!

JUST DITCH COACH JOHN AND ASK SOMEONE **ELSE**!
CH

FINE. IS YOUR FATHER AVAILABLE?
ACH

THIS GUY'S BEGINNING TO GROW ON ME.
Peirce

HI, GRAMPS!
WELL! HELLO, BOY!

NATE, YOU REMEMBER MY NEIGHBORS, CHARLIE AND STAN!
YUP! HI!

BEEN PLAYING BASEBALL, SON?
YUP! WE JUST HAD PRACTICE!
AND LET ME TELL YOU, HE'S **GOOD**!

HE'S A SOLID HITTER! HE CAN HIT TO ALL FIELDS! AND HE'S A FAST BASERUNNER, TOO!

AND HE PLAYS THE OUTFIELD THE WAY IT'S **MEANT** TO BE PLAYED! PLUS, HE'S GOT THE BEST THROWING ARM ON THE TEAM!

YOU KNOW WHAT'S CUTE? HIS TEAM IS CALLED THE **CUPCAKES!**

MMPH!... HEH HEH! HA HA HA HA HA HEH HEH HA HA HA

HA HA HA HA HA HA HA HA
WELL, IT **IS** CUTE!
IT'S ADORABLE.
Peirce

HEY, WANNA HIT THE ARCADE AFTER SCHOOL?
SORRY, TEDDY. I DON'T HAVE ANY MONEY.

PLUS, MY DAD'S MAKING ME GO TO THE BARBERSHOP.
WAIT, SO YOU **DO** HAVE MONEY!

YEAH, MONEY FOR A **HAIRCUT.**
HEY, I JUST THOUGHT OF SOME-THING!

THE BEGINNING OF A VERY VERY VERY VERY VERY BAD IDEA
WHAT IF... ?

YOU'LL CUT MY HAIR?
YEAH! SO YOU CAN USE YOUR HAIR-CUT MONEY FOR THE ARCADE!

MY MOM'S GOT ONE OF THOSE DO-IT-YOURSELF BARBER KITS! SHE USES IT ON ME ALL THE TIME!

YOUR DAD GAVE YOU MONEY FOR A HAIRCUT! IT'S NOT LIKE HE CARES WHERE YOU GET IT CUT!
TEDDY, THAT'S... THATS...

THE MYSTERIOUS LOGIC OF THE PRE-ADOLESCENT BRAIN
THAT'S GENIUS!
YES, I KNOW.
Peirce

MAN! I CAN'T BELIEVE HOW FAST I WENT THROUGH MY HAIRCUT MONEY!
YEAH, THAT WAS CRAZY.

BUT AREN'T YOU GLAD YOU SPENT IT AT THE ARCADE INSTEAD OF PAYING IT TO SOME CRUSTY OLD BARBER?
DEFINITELY!

SPEAKING OF BARBERS, HOW MANY HAIRCUTS HAVE YOU DONE BESIDES ME?
NONE.

EARLY WARNING SIGN
BUT HOW HARD CAN IT BE?

HERE, PUT THIS ON SO YOU DON'T GET HAIR ALL OVER YOUR CLOTHES.

THIS IS MY MOM'S BARBER KIT!
WOW, IT'S LIKE A **DELUXE** SET!

LOOK AT ALL THOSE PLASTIC ATTACHMENTS.
YEAH, BUT MY MOM DOESN'T USE THEM.

OMINOUS FORESHADOWING
SHE SAYS THOSE ARE FOR AMATEURS!
BZZZZZZ
Peirce

WELL? START CUTTING!
YEAH, YEAH. I WILL.
BZZZZZZ

BUT... I JUST DON'T THINK I COULD LIVE WITH MYSELF IF I DIDN'T SAY SOMETHING FIRST.

YOU HAVE INCREDIBLY WEIRD HAIR, DUDE.

BARBERSHOP DISHARMONY
YOU KNOW HOW PEOPLE SAY BARBERS TALK TOO MUCH?
IT'S LIKE A FUZZY PALM TREE!
Peirce

OKAY, READY? I'M GONNA START IN BACK AND WORK MY WAY UP TO THE FRONT!
BZZZZZZ

BZZZZZZZZZZZZZZ

BZZZZZZZZZWANNG.

RED ALERT
WHOOPS.
WHAT WHOOPS? **WHAT WHOOPS?**
Peirce

WHAT'S HAPPENING? DID YOU MESS UP?
NO! NO! JUST HOLD STILL!
BZZZ

BZZZONK!
PLOP!

D-DID MY HAIR JUST HIT THE FLOOR WITH AN AUDIBLE "PLOP"?

IT MIGHT HAVE.
HAIR IS NOT SUP-POSED TO MAKE NOISE!!
Peirce

TEDDY, WHAT'S GOING ON BACK THERE? ARE YOU BUTCHERING MY HAIR?
NO! NO! IT'S... UH... A LITTLE UNEVEN, THAT'S ALL.

WELL, **EVEN IT UP**, THEN!
OKAY, OKAY. HANG ON.
BZZZZZ

BZZZ
Z
ZOW!

IT'S EVEN, BUT IT LOOKS ODD.
GET ME A MIRROR! GET ME A MIRROR!
Peirce

GAAH! WHAT DID YOU DO?
SORRY SORRY SORRY

I'M BALD!
IT'S NOT THAT BAD! IT REALLY ISN'T!

I LOOK LIKE SOME SORT OF DERANGED CHIA PET!
NO, YOU DON'T! NOT AT ALL!

CHIA PETS ARE GREEN!
YAAAAH!
Peirce

THANKS A LOT, TEDDY! WHAT KIND OF A BARBER ARE YOU?

YOU MADE ME LOOK LIKE A DOOFUS! I'LL BE A LAUGHING-STOCK! MY LIFE IS RUINED!

SLAM!

I GUESS HOPING FOR A TIP MIGHT HAVE BEEN A BIT OPTIMISTIC.
peirce

I'M HOME.
HI, NATE! HOW WAS SCHOOL?

OH, AND WHAT ABOUT THE BARBERSHOP? DID YOU GET A HAIRCUT?

NATE? DID YOU GET A HAIRCUT?

I GOT 'EM ALL CUT.
SWEET STICKY MOLASSES!
! ! !

YOUR... YOUR HAIR!
I KNOW, I KNOW. LIKE AN IDIOT, I LET TEDDY CUT IT.

SO GO AHEAD AND SAY IT. TELL ME HOW BAD IT LOOKS. I CAN TAKE IT.

I...I...

I LOVE IT!
IT'S WORSE THAN I THOUGHT.

WHAT A GORGEOUS DAY FOR A WALK!
OH, NO. HERE COMES DOTTIE.

I REFUSE TO STAND HERE FOR AN HOUR LISTENING TO HER NONSTOP YAKKING!

NOW, VERN, DON'T SAY ANYTHING RUDE!
LEAVE THIS TO ME, MARGE. I WON'T SPEAK A WORD.

HELLO, YOU TWO! OH, MY GOODNESS, IT'S BEEN AGES!

I HAVEN'T SEEN YOU SINCE BILL AND I GOT BACK FROM OUR CRUISE! OH, WHAT A TIME WE HAD!

OF COURSE, WE SIMPLY ADORE THE TROPICS, AND-
URK!

GNK!
AGH!

OH, DEAR! HE'S HAVING ONE OF HIS SPELLS! I NEED TO GET HIM HOME! BYE, DOTTIE!

AS I WAS SAYING, IT'S A GORGEOUS DAY FOR A WALK!
YOU'RE WELCOME.

I'M SERIOUS, NATE! I THINK YOUR NEW 'DO LOOKS GREAT! SHORT HAIR NEVER GOES OUT OF STYLE!

IT'S CLASSIC! IT'S TIMELESS! IT'LL DRIVE THE LADIES WILD!
THE LADIES? SURE, DAD.

"HI, NATE, NICE SHIRT!" "HI, NATE, NICE PANTS!"...

"HI, NATE, NICE SCALP!"
HE'S A HEAD CASE.

NO! **NOBODY'S** GONNA SEE! THAT'S WHY I BANDAGED MYSELF LIKE THIS! I'M GONNA TELL EVERYONE I HAVE A BAD HEAD INJURY!

WELL, IF IT ISN'T THE **BUTCHER** HIMSELF!
OH, COME ON. I SAID I WAS SORRY!

SORRY ISN'T **GOOD** ENOUGH, TEDDY! YOU TOTALLY DESTROYED MY HAIR!

...AND MY HAIR IS MY BEST FEATURE!
MMPH!

REALLY?
SADLY ENOUGH, THAT'S PROBABLY TRUE!
ZIP IT.

WOWZA! NATE! WHAT **HAP-PENED**?
ER... HEAD INJURY, CHAD.

BUT YOU'RE OKAY, THOUGH, RIGHT?
YEAH.

HEY, **HERE'S** SOME-THING FUNNY! WHEN I SAW YOU WITH YOUR HEAD ALL WRAPPED UP, YOU KNOW WHAT I THOUGHT?

I THOUGHT YOU MIGHT BE COVERING UP A TERRIBLE HAIRCUT! HA HA!
HA.
Peirce

NATE, TAKE OFF THAT RIDICULOUS HAT.
IT'S NOT A HAT, MRS. GODFREY! IT'S A **BANDAGE!**

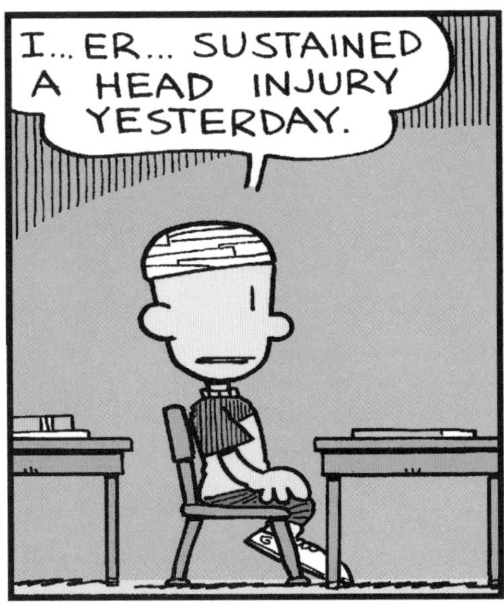
I... ER... SUSTAINED A HEAD INJURY YESTERDAY.

WHAT KIND OF HEAD INJURY?
UM... A SERIOUS ONE.

SO SERIOUS, I WASN'T ABLE TO DO THE HOMEWORK.
HE'S DOUBLING DOWN.

DON'T YOU FEEL KIND OF STUPID, WEARING A BANDAGE ON YOUR HEAD FOR NO REASON?
IT'S **NOT** FOR NO REASON!

IT'S BECAUSE **SOME-BODY** GAVE ME A HAIRCUT THAT MAKES ME LOOK LIKE A **SKINHEAD**!

SO **EXCUSE** ME FOR NOT WANTING EVERY-BODY TO **LAUGH** AT ME!

THIS WAY, I DON'T ATTRACT ANY ATTENTION!
HEY, WHO'S THE DORK IN THE TURBAN?
HA HA HA HA
Peirce

Y'KNOW, FRANCIS, YOU'RE RIGHT! I FEEL RIDICULOUS WEARING THIS STUPID BANDAGE!

IF PEOPLE WANT TO LOOK AT ME, THERE'S NOTHING I CAN DO ABOUT IT! THEY CAN GO AHEAD AND LOOK AT ME!

HEAR THAT, EVERY-BODY? GO AHEAD AND LOOK AT ME! **LOOK AT ME!**

WHY AREN'T THEY LOOKING AT ME?
YOU'RE NOT THAT INTERESTING.
Peirce

SEE, I **TOLD** YOU HAVING SHORT HAIR WOULDN'T BE THAT BAD!
I GUESS YOU'RE RIGHT.

THERE MIGHT EVEN BE SOME UNEXPECTED BENEFITS!
LIKE WHAT?

HI, NATE, CAN I RUB YOUR HEAD?

HEY, GIRLS! COME FEEL HOW FUZZY!
OH, BROTHER.
peirce

GOODNESS, NATE, THAT'S QUITE A HAIRCUT!
IT WASN'T EXACTLY INTENTIONAL.

WELL, I'D LET IT GROW BACK AS SOON AS POSSIBLE.

YOU DON'T SERVE A HEAD OF LETTUCE LIKE YOURS ON THE SIDE, CHILD. YOU MAKE IT THE MAIN COURSE.
For Gramm

MRS. SHIPULSKI LIKES MY LETTUCE!
HA HA! I HAVE NO IDEA WHAT THAT MEANS!
Peirce

HAS ANYONE MADE FUN OF YOUR HAIRCUT, NATE?

YEAH, A FEW PEOPLE HAVE...

HEY, CURLY! DID YOU CUT YOUR HAIR WITH A **WEED WHACKER**?

FIVE SECONDS LATER...
...BUT I'VE COME UP WITH AN APPROPRIATE RESPONSE!
YAY!
Peirce

DO YOU FEEL WEAK WITH SHORT HAIR?
WHATTA YA MEAN?

LIKE SAMSON! WITHOUT HIS HAIR, HE LOST HIS STRENGTH.
HMM. LEMME SEE.

TEDDY, YO MAMA'S SO FAT, THERE ARE MILE MARKERS ON HER PANTYHOSE.

NOPE, I'VE STILL GOT IT.
PEIRCE

YOUR HAIR'S GROWING BACK PRETTY QUICKLY!
YUP!

I'M HANDING BACK YOUR TESTS, PEOPLE!

POINK!

I THINK YOU JUST ADDED AN INCH!
OH, HOW I HATE SOCIAL STUDIES.

NICE DOGGIE... GIVE ME THE FRISBEE, OKAY? GOOOOD BOY...
GRRRRRRRRR

ROWR! ROWF! GROWF! WORF!

HALLO, DOG. YOU WILL GIVE TO ME FRISBEE? PLEASE?
GRRRR RRRRR RRRR

RARF! RARF! RARF! RARF!

HEY, THERE, FELLA... CAN I HAVE THAT? NIIIICE DOG...
RRRRRRR...

RAFF! RARF! WORF! RORF! GROWF!!

BEHOLD THE POWER OF CHAD!
YOU GUYS WANNA PLAY FRISBEE?

DING
DONG

WELL, HI THERE, SPITSY!
URF!

NATE'S NOT HERE, IF YOU'RE LOOKING FOR A PLAYMATE!

AW. SORRY, BOY. I CAN SEE YOU'RE DISAPPOINTED.

...BUT HEY!
I CAN TOSS YOU THE BALL!
WURF!

GO GET IT, SPITSY!
ZING!

SPITSY?

SPITSY?
CLICK!

RATTLE
RATTLE
RATTLE

Peirce

NATE, I'VE GOT TO RUN TO THE BANK. I'LL BE BACK IN TEN MINUTES. YOU'RE IN CHARGE.
TEN-FOUR, GORDIE!

WOW! THAT'S PRETTY COOL! I'M IN CHARGE OF THE STORE!

I'VE GOT THE WHOLE PLACE TO MYSELF! IT'S JUST ME AND...

...RANDY!
MARVEL
STAFF PICKS

UGH! IT'S RANDY! MR. BIG MAN ON CAMPUS!
MANGA

I'VE NEVER SEEN HIM HERE BEFORE! I'M PRETTY SURE HE DOESN'T EVEN **LIKE** COMICS!

SO WHAT'S HE DOING HERE?

LAZY
IDEA MAN
JUVENILE TITLES

!! I THINK RANDY JUST STUFFED A COMIC BOOK IN HIS JACKET!
...OR **DID** HE?
AMY
KLIK!
GRADY
MICRO-
Lunk
OCEAN
SILENT

IT'S HARD TO BE SURE WITH HIS BACK TURNED.
IF I ACCUSE HIM, HE'LL PROBABLY PUNCH MY **FACE** IN!

AMY
KLIK!
GRADY
MICRO-
Lunk
OCEAN

WHAT WOULD **YOU** DO?

I'M ALMOST POSITIVE RANDY'S TRYING TO STEAL A COMIC BOOK! BUT WHAT DO I **DO** ABOUT IT?
KLIK!
GRADY
MICRO-
Lunk
OCEAN
SILENT IN

I GUESS I'LL JUST WAIT IT OUT. GORDIE WILL BE BACK SOON, AND THEN I CAN—
KLIK!
BONUS DOUBLE ISSUE!
SOCIETY
Lunk
OCEAN

!! HE'S LEAVING THE STORE!
AMY
KLIK!
GRADY
MICRO-
Lunk
OCEAN
SILENT IN

FREEZE!

HOLD IT, RANDY!
WHAT ARE YOU DOING HERE, SCRUB?

I WORK HERE. AND I JUST SAW YOU STEAL A COMIC BOOK!
I DON'T KNOW WHAT YOU'RE TALKING ABOUT!

IT'S INSIDE YOUR JACKET!
WHAT'S INSIDE MY JACKET? YOU'RE CRAZY!

WHUMP!
Peirce

GORDIE!
OH! HEY, DIEGO!

I'M ON BREAK! WANNA GRAB A COFFEE AT THE FOOD COURT?
CAN'T.

I'VE GOT TO GET BACK TO THE STORE! I LEFT OUR ELEVEN-YEAR-OLD INTERN IN CHARGE!

WHAT THE-?
I NEED A MALL COP!
SIC
IX

WHAT IS GOING ON?
GORDIE! I CAUGHT A SHOPLIFTER!

I'M NOT A SHOPLIFTER!
YES, HE IS! I SAW HIM!

OPEN UP HIS JACKET! YOU'LL FIND A COMIC BOOK!

WHAT COMIC BOOK?

SORRY, NATE. LOOKS LIKE YOUR SHOPLIFTER'S **NOT** A SHOPLIFTER.
BUT I **SAW** IT!

I APOLOGIZE FOR THE MISUNDERSTANDING, YOUNG MAN.
NO BIGGIE. WELL, GUESS I'LL GET GOING.

NATE? DON'T **YOU** HAVE SOMETHING TO SAY?
!

WHUMP!
Peirce

LEMME GO!
NATE! WHAT ARE YOU DOING?
KL
K

HE'S ALREADY PROVEN HE DIDN'T TAKE ANYTHING!
YES, HE DID! IT'S UP HIS SLEEVE!

AH-HA! SEE? I TOLD YOU HE STOLE A COMIC BOO—! WAIT, HOLD ON...

YOU SHOP-LIFTED "MY LITTLE PONY: PINKIE PIE KEEPS A SECRET"?
THE PLOT THICKENS.

HEH HEH! HOW COME YOU TRIED TO STEAL A "MY LITTLE PONY" BOOK, RANDY?
SHUT UP, OKAY? I KNOW IT LOOKS STUPID.

I NEEDED A GIFT FOR MY COUSIN'S BIRTHDAY, AND I DIDN'T HAVE ANY MONEY!

HMM... NATE, WHAT DO YOU THINK WE SHOULD DO WITH OUR FRIEND HERE?

YOU MEAN IT'S UP TO **ME**?
UH, NO.
peirce

AH! WAYNE, YOU'RE BACK! WE'VE GOT A SITUATION HERE. NATE CAUGHT A SHOPLIFTER.

HOW DO YOU WANT TO HANDLE IT?
MUMBLE MUMBLE MUMBLE MUMBLE MUMBLE

W-WHAT DID HE SAY?
HA! WOULDN'T YOU LIKE TO KNOW!

YEAH, I **WOULD**!
SO WOULD I, ACTUALLY.
Peirce

OKAY, UH... RANDY, IS IT? THIS BOOK YOU TRIED TO STEAL HAS BEEN DAMAGED. SO IT'S YOURS. BUT YOU'LL HAVE TO BUY IT.
BUT I HAVE NO MONEY!

WE'LL GIVE YOU A WEEK. IF YOU HAVEN'T PAID FOR IT BY THEN, WE'LL HAVE TO INFORM YOUR PARENTS ABOUT THIS INCIDENT.

AND BEFORE YOU GO, YOU SHOULD THANK NATE FOR STOPPING YOU BEFORE YOU COULD GO THROUGH WITH IT.

YOU'RE WELCOME.
KLASSIC KOMIX
Peirce

NATE, YOU DID A GREAT JOB CATCHING RANDY IN THE ACT...
KLA
inky

... BUT NEXT TIME, DON'T **TACKLE** THE SHOPLIFTER!
WELL, WHAT WAS I **SUPPOSED** TO DO?

CALL A **MALL COP!** THERE ARE THREE OF THEM ON PATROL AT ALL TIMES!

UNIT ONE TO UNIT THREE... COUGAR SIGHTING AT "RED MANGO"...
SEE? THERE'S ONE NOW!
SCHOOL PICTURE GUY!
peirce

SCHOOL PICTURE GUY! YOU'RE A MALL COP?
ON DUTY AND AT YOUR SERVICE, AMIGO!

WELL, WHERE WERE YOU A HALF HOUR AGO, WHEN I WAS IN THE MIDDLE OF CATCHING A SHOPLIFTER?

I WAS SHOUTING "I NEED A MALL COP" AS LOUD AS I COULD!
AH. YES, I HEARD THAT.

AND...?
KID, A MAN'S MID-AFTERNOON "CINNABON" BREAK IS A SACRED THING.
Peirce

SCHOOL PICTURE GUY, I HAD NO IDEA YOU WERE A **MALL COP**!
YUP! BEEN WALKIN' THE BEAT FOR A FEW WEEKS NOW!

AND I MUST SAY, I'VE FOUND MY CALLING! I'VE ALWAYS BEEN A PEACEMAKER! A PROTECTOR FOR THOSE WHO NEED PROTECTION!

THE WORLD NEEDS HEROES, M'BOY! WHEN PEOPLE LOOK AT THIS UNIFORM, A HERO IS PRECISELY WHAT THEY SEE!

HEY, FATS, WHICH WAY TO THE RESTROOMS?
STRAIGHT AHEAD, THEN HANG A LEFT AT "DRESS BARN."
Peirce

SO THIS IS YOUR JOB? WALKING AROUND THE MALL ALL DAY?
IT'S NOT JUST WALKING AROUND, AMIGO!

IT'S **OBSERVATION**! EVEN AS WE SPEAK, I'M SCANNING OUR SURROUNDINGS FOR ANYTHING OUT OF THE ORDINARY!

REMEMBER, I'M A PHOTOGRAPHER! I'M TRAINED TO NOTICE THE TINIEST DETAIL! NOTHING ESCAPES MY EAGLE EYE!

ATTENTION ALL UNITS: TWO-FOR-ONE SPECIAL AT "MRS. FIELDS COOKIES."
ON MY WAY.
Peirce

OFFICER, THAT MAN OVER THERE WON'T STOP ANNOYING ME.
AH! LEAVE THIS TO ME, DEAR LADY!

SIR, WHY WON'T YOU LEAVE THIS LOVELY LADY ALONE?

BECAUSE I'M MARRIED TO THE WOMAN.

...FOR **NOW.**
THIS MAY BE ABOVE MY PAY GRADE, MA'AM.
USE YOUR PEPPER SPRAY.
Peirce

HEY, THERE'S ANOTHER MALL COP.
YUP. THAT'S UNIT TWO.

SO YOU GUYS KNOW EACH OTHER?
KNOW EACH OTHER? WE'RE A **TEAM,** KID! A WELL-OILED **MACHINE!!**

WE'RE IN CONSTANT COMMUNICATION! SHARING INTEL IS A VITAL PART OF THIS JOB!

INTEL?
UNIT TWO TO UNIT ONE... HOT NEW MANNEQUIN AT "FASHION BUG."
ROGER THAT.
Peirce

WELL! NOT A BAD DAY AT KLASSIC KOMIX!

IT'S NOT EVERY DAY I GET TO BUST THAT PINHEAD **RANDY** FOR **SHOPLIFTING!**

I'LL NEVER FORGET THE LOOK ON HIS FACE WHEN I APPEARED OUT OF **NOWHERE!**

HEY.
! !

WHAT DO **YOU** WANT, RANDY?
FOR YOU TO KEEP **QUIET**, THAT'S WHAT!

DON'T TELL ANYBODY I **SHOPLIFTED**... OR I'LL REARRANGE YOUR **FACE**!

WELL... SINCE YOU PUT IT **THAT** WAY...

FORGET IT.

HEY! DIDN'T YOU **HEAR** ME? I SAID IF YOU TELL ANYONE I SHOP-LIFTED, I'LL **POUND** YOU!
YEAH, I HEARD YOU.

...BUT SO **WHAT**? YOU **ALREADY** PICK ON ME EVERY **DAY**! ALL YOU'RE DOING IS THREATENING TO KEEP ACTING THE WAY YOU **ALWAYS** ACT!

BUT I **TOLD** YOU—
BOSSING ME AROUND WON'T **WORK**, RANDY!

TRY **ASKING**.
Peirce

YOU WANT ME TO **ASK?** FINE! I'LL **ASK**!

PLEASE DON'T TELL ANYBODY THAT I SHOPLIFTED.
I WILL NEVER TELL ANYBODY THAT YOU SHOPLIFTED.

...AND IN RETURN, **YOU** WILL NEVER WEDGIE ME, NOOGIE ME, PUNCH ME, TRIP ME, KICK ME, OR SHOVE ME INSIDE A LOCKER **EVER AGAIN**.

SAY **WHAT**?
TAKE IT OR LEAVE IT.
Peirce

SO YOU PROMISE NOT TO SPILL THE BEANS ABOUT ME SHOPLIFTING...

...AND **YOU** PROMISE NOT TO WEDGIE, NOOGIE, PUNCH, TRIP, KICK, ELBOW, TACKLE, OR LOCKERIZE ME.

SHAKE ON IT.
OH, AND NO AGGRESSIVELY FIRM HAND-SHAKES.

RATS.
THAT'S PERFECT! NICE 'N FEEBLE!

IT'S A DEAL.
WELL, IF IT ISN'T PUBLIC ENEMY NUMBER ONE! HEY, RANDY! MY SISTER WAS JUST AT THE MALL!

...AND SHE SAW YOU GET CAUGHT TRYING TO SWIPE A MY LITTLE PONY BOOK!
IT'S ALREADY ALL OVER FACE-BOOK!
HA HA
HA HA
HA

THE DEAL'S OFF.
SHOVE!

I THINK THAT WAS WHAT'S KNOWN AS A FRAGILE PEACE.

LAST DAY OF SCHOOL!
YUP! PRANK DAY!
WRIGHT

I WISH I WERE AS GOOD AT PRANKING AS **YOU** ARE.
WELL, IF YOU **WERE** GOOD AT PRANKING, WHO WOULD YOU PRANK?

THE CROSSING GUARD IN FRONT OF THE SCHOOL. HE ALWAYS YELLS AT ME.

STOP
THAT GUY?
YUP.

YOU GO AHEAD, CHAD. I'LL CATCH UP.
? ?

STOP
COME **ON**, SPEEDY! I DON'T HAVE ALL DAY!

WAP! WAP! WAP!
WAP! WAP! WAP!
STOP

THAT'S THE NICEST THING ANY-ONE'S EVER DONE FOR ME!
YOU CAN ACCOMPLISH A LOT WITH A DRONE AND SOME WATER BALLOONS!

I'M GOING TO TRY THE OL' PENCIL TRICK ON SARAH.
WHAT'S THE OL' PENCIL TRICK?

WATCH AND LEARN, CHAD, M'BOY! WATCH AND LEARN!
'KAY!

PLINK!

SARAH! YOU DROPPED YOUR PENCIL!
HM?

HERE YOU GO.
THAT ISN'T MY PENCIL.

THAT HAS **TEETH MARKS** ALL OVER IT! I WOULD **NEVER** CHEW A PENCIL! THAT'S **GROSS**!

THAT'S PROBABLY **YOUR** PENCIL! **YOU** CHEW ON PENCILS ALL THE **TIME**!

I'M WATCHING, BUT I'M NOT LEARNING ANYTHING.
CHEW CHEW CHEW CHEW

I'M GONNA TRY THE OL' PENCIL TRICK AGAIN, CHAD!
WHY?

IT DIDN'T WORK AT **ALL** WITH SARAH!
THAT'S BECAUSE I USED IT ON THE WRONG GIRL! SARAH WAS **ON** TO ME!

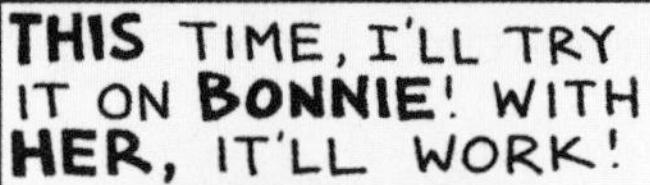
THIS TIME, I'LL TRY IT ON **BONNIE**! WITH **HER**, IT'LL WORK!

WATCH CLOSELY, CHAD! THIS IS HOW IT'S **SUPPOSED** TO BE DONE!

PLINK!

BONNIE! YOU DROPPED YOUR PENCIL!
OH!

CLONK!

I'M SO CONFUSED.
SO AM I, BUT I THINK THAT'S THE CONCUSSION TALKING.
Peirce

LAST DAY OF SCHOOL! I HOPE THE KIDS DON'T GO CRAZY WITH THE USUAL **PRANK DAY** NONSENSE!

I DON'T WANT TO DEAL WITH TURTLES IN THE TOILET BOWLS, STINK BOMBS IN THE TEACHERS' LOUNGE...

THERE'S QUICKSAND IN THE PARKING LOT.
YEAH. WOW. FREAKY.
Peirce

NATE, WHAT DO YOU KNOW ABOUT THIS?
ABOUT WHAT?

ABOUT THE FACT THAT A SINKHOLE FULL OF **QUICKSAND** HAS SUDDENLY APPEARED ON **SCHOOL GROUNDS**!

WHA-? HEY, **WAIT** A MINUTE! THIS ACTUALLY ISN'T QUICKSAND AT **ALL**!

THIS IS **CREAM OF WHEAT**!
COOL. WANT ME TO GET YOU A SPOON?
Peirce

I HEARD PRINCIPAL NICHOLS FELL INTO A SINKHOLE IN THE PARKING LOT THIS MORNING.

I ALSO HEARD THAT SOMEBODY FILLED THE SINKHOLE WITH **CREAM OF WHEAT!**

CREAM OF WHEAT, HUH?
OBVIOUSLY THE WORK OF A "CEREAL" PRANKSTER!

WA HAHAHA HA HA HA HA HA
Peirce

YOU COULD GET BUSTED FOR THAT SINKHOLE PRANK, NATE. THERE ARE SECURITY CAMERAS IN THE PARKING LOT.

WHAT IF PRINCIPAL NICHOLS REVIEWS THE FOOTAGE AND SEES **YOU**?

WHAT IF ALL THE FOOTAGE HAS BEEN REPLACED WITH SEASON THREE OF "DANCE MOMS"?

WHAT THE-?
FOCUS, CHLOE! YOU WANT A SOLO OR **NOT**?
SOB!
Peirce

ALL RIGHT, PEOPLE, I HEARD ABOUT THE **SINKHOLE** IN THE PARKING LOT THIS MORNING!

I CAN ASSURE YOU, I WILL TOLERATE NO PRANK DAY HIJINKS IN **THIS**—
SUMO-GRAM!

SUMOGRAM FOR MRS. GODFREY!

"ROSES ARE RED, VIOLETS ARE BLUE. RETIRE FROM YOUR JOB AND MOVE TO PERU."
CRIPES.
PEIRCE

LINE UP, WEAKLINGS! IT MAY BE THE LAST DAY OF SCHOOL, BUT THAT DOESN'T MEAN YOU CAN WEASEL OUT OF WIND SPRINTS!

FLAP
FLAP
FLAP
FLAP
FLAP

SNAG!

HA HA HA HA HA
HA HA
WHERE'D YOU GET THE FALCON?
I KNOW A GUY.
HA HA
Peirce

NATE, YOUR REPORT CARD SIMPLY ISN'T ACCEPTABLE.

LOOK AT YOUR SISTER! ELLEN WORKS HARD IN SCHOOL, AND SHE'S REWARDED WITH GOOD GRADES!

YOU'RE CERTAINLY CAPABLE OF DOING THE SAME THING, SINCE YOU HAVE A HIGHER...UH...

WHOOPS.
A HIGHER WHAT?? A HIGHER WHAT??
Peirce

YOU **STOPPED** YOURSELF BECAUSE PARENTS ALWAYS HAVE TO **PRETEND** THEIR KIDS ARE EXACTLY THE **SAME**!

WHAT'S THIS ALL ABOUT?
OUR I.Q.'s, ELLEN! THAT'S WHAT!

DAD WAS JUST ABOUT TO SPILL THE BEANS THAT I'M OFFICIALLY SMARTER THAN YOU!

HUH? IS THAT TRUE?

UH...
ACCEPT IT, ELLEN! YOU GOT THE BIG BED-ROOM, I GOT THE BIG BRAIN!
Peirce

ALL RIGHT, I'LL TELL YOU: YES, BOTH OF YOU TOOK AN I.Q. TEST WHEN YOU WERE QUITE YOUNG.

...AND NATE, YOUR I.Q. IS JUST **SLIGHTLY** HIGHER THAN ELLEN'S.

IN FACT, BELIEVE IT OR NOT... *CHUCKLE!*... YOUR I.Q. IS HIGHER THAN **MINE**, TOO!
WELL, **DUH!**

WHAT?
I MEAN, TELL ME SOMETHING I **DIDN'T** KNOW, RIGHT?
PEIRCE

SO, ELLEN, HOW'S IT FEEL TO BE THE... *AHEM!*... **SECOND** SMARTEST KID IN THE FAMILY?
WHO CARES?

I.Q. IS ONLY **ONE** KIND OF INTELLIGENCE, YOU KNOW! THERE'S COMMON SENSE! MATURITY! SAGACITY!

TIK
TIK
TIK

YOU'RE GOOGLING "SAGACITY," AREN'T YOU?
WHO, ME?

SO, DAD... WHAT **IS** MY I.Q.?
IT'S A VERY RESPECTABLE NUMBER.

WELL, HOW MUCH DID I BEAT ELLEN BY?
NATE, IT'S NOT A **CONTEST**.

WHAT MATTERS IS WHAT YOU DO WITH THE GIFTS YOU'RE GIVEN.
I GET **GIFTS**?

NOT FOR THE FORESEEABLE FUTURE.
CAN I HAVE ONE OF THOSE MASSAGE CHAIRS?

WELL, HI THERE, SPITSY! LOOKING FOR NATE?
WURF!

HE'S NOT HERE! HE'S WORKING AT THE COMICS STORE!

WHIMPER

OWOOO

SPITSY! SPITSY! CALM DOWN! TAKE IT EASY!
OWOOO

I'LL PLAY WITH YOU!
WURF?

SURE I WILL! JUST TELL ME WHAT YOU WANT TO PLAY!

WHISPER
WHISPER
WHISPER
WHISPER
WHISPER
WHISPER
WHISPER

I'M OKAY WITH THE TEA PARTY, BUT I DRAW THE LINE AT THE LIVE STREAM.
Peirce

HEY. I NEED TO SELL THIS COMIC BOOK.
LET'S TAKE A LOOK.

HMMM...

WE'LL PAY YOU FORTY DOLLARS FOR IT.
FORTY BUCKS?

NICE TRY, JUNIOR! IT'S WORTH TEN TIMES THAT!!

GET SOMEONE OUT HERE WHO KNOWS WHAT HE'S DOING!
WHATEVER YOU SAY.

WAYNE!

NOW WE'RE GETTING SOMEWHERE!
WHAT'S THIS WORTH?

MUMBLE MUMBLE MUMBLE MUMBLE

HE SAID IT'S WORTH FORTY DOLLARS...

... IN PENNIES.
WUMP!

...AND THEN HE SAID: "HAVE A NICE DAY."

YOU AND I ARE TOSSING A FRISBEE, SEE... BUT THEN ONE OF YOUR THROWS GOES AWRY, LANDING AT THE FEET OF LUISA, A RAVEN-HAIRED EXCHANGE STUDENT FROM BARCELONA.

OUR EYES MEET AS SHE SHYLY HANDS ME BACK THE FRISBEE, AND A SPARK IS KINDLED! SHE SPEAKS NO ENGLISH, BUT THAT DOESN'T MATTER BECAUSE—

SO YOU'RE LOOKING FOR A NEW GIRL-FRIEND, HUH?
NO, NOT A GIRLFRIEND. A SUMMER ROMANCE!

YOU KNOW, THE SORT OF THING WHERE EVEN THOUGH SHE AND I ARE CRAZY ABOUT EACH OTHER, OUR RELATION-SHIP IS DOOMED TO FAIL BECAUSE WE'RE FROM TWO DIFFERENT WORLDS!

LOOK AROUND, TEDDY! WHICH GIRLS LOOK LIKE THEIR ROMANCE WITH ME WOULD BE DOOMED TO FAIL?

ALL OF THEM!
SHUT UP.

HI, GUYS!
DEE DEE! QUESTION FOR YOU:

LOOK AROUND AND TELL ME IF YOU SEE A GOOD CANDIDATE FOR A SUMMER ROMANCE!
OKAY...

OOH! RIGHT **THERE**!

HI, SAILOR.
TSK! Y'KNOW HOW SOME PEOPLE THINK ONLY OF THEMSELVES?
GEE, WHAT'S THAT LIKE?
Peirce

SEE THAT GIRL OVER THERE IN THE RED BATHING SUIT?

WHAT A HOTTIE, RIGHT? SHE'S THE PERFECT SUMMER ROMANCE!

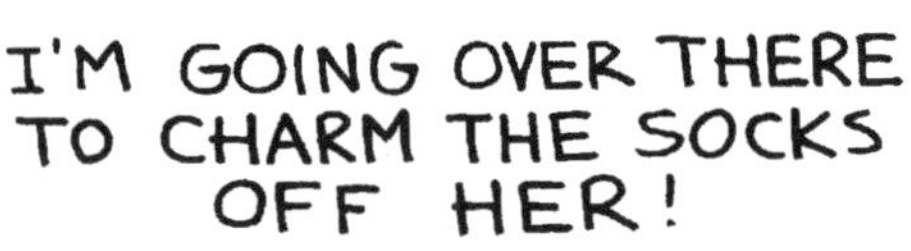
I'M GOING OVER THERE TO CHARM THE SOCKS OFF HER!

WHAT ABOUT THE GUY RUBBING SUNBLOCK ON HER BACK?
HE CAN PUT SOME ON ME, TOO. I'M STARTING TO GET A LITTLE PINK.

NATE, THAT GIRL YOU WANT TO HAVE A SUMMER ROMANCE WITH CLEARLY HAS A BOYFRIEND!
WHO SAYS?

JUST BECAUSE SOME GUY'S RUBBING SUNBLOCK ON HER DOESN'T MEAN HE'S HER BOYFRIEND! HE'S PROBABLY HER COUSIN! OR HER BROTHER!

CLOSE FAMILY.
RATS. OKAY, I'M MOVING ON TO PLAN B.

WELL, I'VE TALKED TO PRACTICALLY EVERY GIRL ON THE BEACH, WITH ABSOLUTELY **NOTHING** TO SHOW FOR IT!

I'M GOING TO **FORGET** ABOUT HAVING A SUMMER ROMANCE! IT'S IMPOSSIBLE TO EVEN **MEET** ANYBODY!

HERE, TEDDY, I GOT US SOME ONION RINGS TO SHARE!

HE'S THE ONE I WAS TELLING YOU ABOUT.
EW.
OH, COME ON!

NATE, THE SCHOOL JUST EMAILED ME YOUR REPORT CARD.

TAKE A LOOK.
ULP!

ARE YOU... UH... MAD?
SIGH... WHAT WOULD BE THE POINT?

MAYBE I **WOULD** GET MAD, IF I THOUGHT IT WOULD MOTIVATE YOU TO TAKE YOUR STUDIES SERIOUSLY...

...BUT YOU'VE MADE IT CLEAR THAT MY CONCERNS ABOUT YOUR SCHOOLWORK MATTER VERY LITTLE TO YOU.

SO AM I MAD? NO, AT THIS STAGE I'M JUST... NUMB.

NUMB IS GOOD!
YOU'RE SO LUCKY, DUDE!
WHAP!
Peirce

HEY! ICE CREAM!
KOOL BEAR

STOP! HEY!

WAIT! SLOW DOWN!

GASP! HEY!

WHEEZE! S-STOP!

WHEW! GASP! I'LL TAKE A—
SORRY, DUDE, MY DAY'S OVER. I'M SOLD OUT.
STOP

WHAT? IF YOU'RE OUT OF ICE CREAM, WHY ARE YOU PLAYING THIS MUSIC?

BECAUSE I LIKE IT, BRO. IT'S CATCHY!
KOOL BEAR

HYPOTHETICALLY, WHAT WOULD BE THE PENALTY FOR VANDALIZING AN ICE CREAM TRUCK?

I'M BROKE. I GOTTA EARN SOME MONEY.
SAME HERE, BUT I DON'T WANT TO MOW LAWNS AGAIN.

HEY! LET'S BE **BUSKERS**!
BUSKERS?
STREET PERFORMERS!

WE'LL PLAY MUSIC ON THE STREET, AND PEOPLE WALKING BY WILL GIVE US MONEY!
YES! "ENSLAVE THE MOLLUSK" WILL **ROCK AGAIN**!

GET YOUR MOTOR RUNNIN'... HEAD OUT ON THE HIGHWAY...
MAYBE PEOPLE WILL PAY US **NOT** TO PLAY.

THE ONLY PROBLEM IS, ARTUR IS ON A FAMILY VACATION, AND HE'S OUR LEAD SINGER! IF ONLY WE COULD FIND SOMEONE TO—

GO GET YOUR INSTRUMENTS, GUYS, AND WE'LL MEET BACK HERE!
OKAY.

ARGH. I LIKE DEE DEE AND EVERYTHING, BUT SHE'S NOT A GREAT SINGER.
SHE SINGS BETTER THAN **YOU** DO!

WHAT ARE YOU IMPLYING?
I'M NOT IMPLYING ANYTHING.

YOU'RE IMPLYING I CAN'T SING.
NO, I'M SAYING IT OUTRIGHT. YOU'RE A TRAIN WRECK.
Peirce

OKAY! I'M READY!
BUT WE CAN'T START BUSKING UNTIL DEE DEE LEARNS ALL OUR **SONGS**!

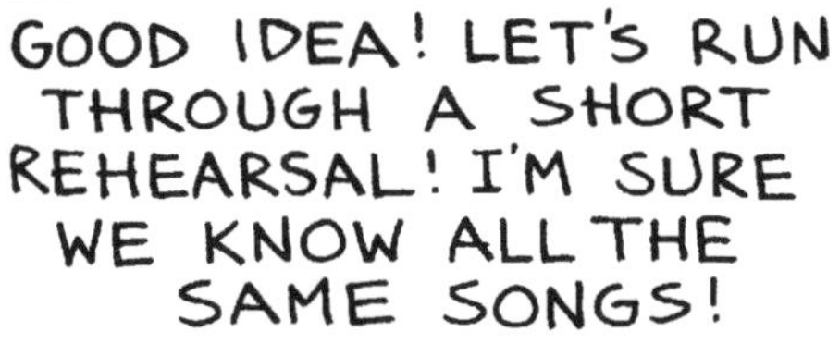
GOOD IDEA! LET'S RUN THROUGH A SHORT REHEARSAL! I'M SURE WE KNOW ALL THE SAME SONGS!

LET'S START WITH "MEMORY" FROM THE ICONIC BROADWAY MUSICAL, "CATS"!

QUICK WARM-UP:
BIP BOO BIPPITY BOO-WAAH!
I DON'T KNOW THIS ONE, SO I'M JUST GONNA PLAY "CHOPSTICKS."
I REFUSE TO PLAY A SONG ABOUT CATS.

IT'S IMPORTANT FOR US TO HAVE A CONSISTENT MUSICAL MESSAGE WHEN WE'RE OUT THERE GIGGING!

HEY, WE'RE STARTING TO SOUND PRETTY GOOD!
I THINK WE'RE READY TO START BUSKING!
Enslave the MOLLUSK

WHERE SHOULD WE GO? WE NEED A GOOD LOCATION.
LET'S HEAD DOWN-TOWN!
Enslave

I HAVE THE PERFECT PLACE IN MIND! IT'S ALWAYS SUPER CROWDED!

MEANWHILE...
MAPLE WALNUT!
I HAVE A MASTER'S DEGREE.
PISTACHIO!
ERMINT!
KIE GH!
BUBBLE GUM!
SWEET LICKS
Peirce

HI, MR. ROSA!
WELCOME TO SWEET LICKS, NATE! WHAT CAN I DO FOR YOU?

WRONG QUESTION! YOU SHOULD BE ASKING WHAT **WE** CAN DO FOR **YOU**!

AND THE **ANSWER** IS: ENSLAVE THE MOLLUSK IS GOING TO GIVE YOU TWO SCOOPS OF **ROCK**!

OH, GOOD.
BUT SINCE YOU ASKED, CAN I HAVE A FREE SAMPLE OF MOCHA FUDGE?
CHOCOLATE
CINNAMON

YOU WANT TO PLAY MUSIC IN FRONT OF THE SHOP?
YUP! RIGHT ON THE SIDEWALK!
F

WELL, I CAN'T MAKE THAT DECISION ON MY OWN, NATE. I'LL HAVE TO ASK THE MANAGER.

WALLY?
FLAVORS
ADD
FRAPPES
• COFFEE
• PEANUTS
YEAH?

THAT'S YOUR MANAGER?
HE'S THE OWNER'S NEPHEW.
I'LL BE SIXTEEN NEXT MONTH.

HEY, THAT GUY JUST THREW SOMETHING IN MY GUITAR CASE!
OOH! HOW MUCH?
Enslave the MOLLUSK

IT'S NOT MONEY. IT'S ONLY AN OLD SKITTLES BAG.
RATS.
Enslave the MOLLUSK

WAIT, ARE THERE ANY SKITTLES LEFT IN IT??

YOU'D EAT **PRE-OWNED SKITTLES?**
UNLESS THEY WERE SOUR APPLE, YES.

WE'VE RUN THROUGH OUR WHOLE SET LIST. WHAT SHOULD WE PLAY NOW?
LET'S TAKE SOME REQUESTS!
Enslave the

DEE DEE! **NO!**
HEY, GIRLS, ANY SONGS YOU'D LIKE TO HEAR?

LET IT GO!
UNDER THE SEA!
BE OUR GUEST!
A WHOLE NEW WORLD!
HOW FAR I'LL GO!

WELCOME TO THE DISNEY-EST PLACE ON EARTH.
A WORLD WITHOUT DRUM SOLOS.
Enslave

HEY! WHO SAID YOU COULD BUSK HERE?
THE ICE CREAM SHOP SAID IT WAS OKAY!

WELL, IT'S NOT! MY BUSKING SPOT IS RIGHT ACROSS THE STREET! YOU'RE CRAMPING MY STYLE!

GO FIND SOMEWHERE ELSE TO PLAY YOUR LITTLE SONGS!

WE'VE JUST BEEN PUNKED BY A FLUTE PLAYER.
HOW HUMILIATING.

SO LONG, MR. ROSA. WE'RE TAKIN' OFF.
YOU'RE DONE BUSKING?
DELI

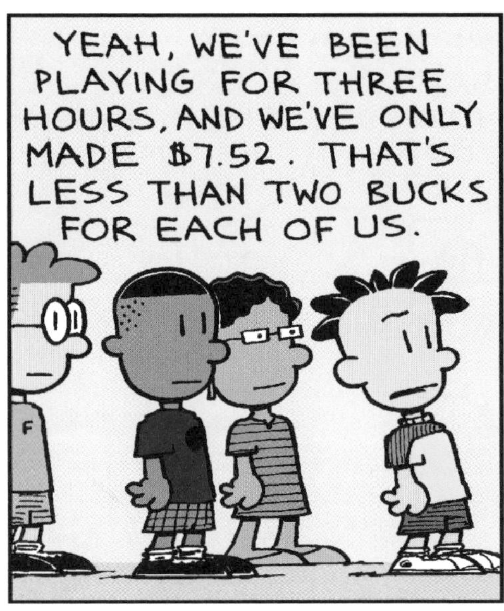
YEAH, WE'VE BEEN PLAYING FOR THREE HOURS, AND WE'VE ONLY MADE $7.52. THAT'S LESS THAN TWO BUCKS FOR EACH OF US.

MEANWHILE, **YOU'RE** MAKING MONEY HAND OVER FIST IN AIR-CONDITIONED **COMFORT**!

THAT'S GOT TO BE THE FIRST TIME MINIMUM WAGE HAS BEEN DESCRIBED AS "HAND OVER FIST."
AND YOU'VE GOT A **TIP JAR**!
PEIRCE

FRANCIS! GOING TO BOOK CLUB AT THE LIBRARY?
UH-HUH.

GREAT! I'LL JOIN YOU!
GROAN...

WHAT WAS **THAT** FOR?
YOU HAVE NO INTEREST IN BOOK CLUB, NATE! YOU JUST WANT TO EAT OUR **SNACKS**!

WHAT'S WRONG WITH **THAT**?
IT'S TOTALLY **DISRUPTIVE**!

IT DOESN'T EXACTLY ENHANCE OUR MEETINGS WHEN YOU STUFF YOUR FACE AND THEN LEAVE AFTER FIVE MINUTES!

IF YOU'RE COMING, YOU HAVE TO STAY FOR THE FULL **HOUR**.
FINE!

STAYING LONGER JUST MEANS I GET TO EAT **MORE**!

THIS WEEK'S BOOK WAS "MY SUGAR-FREE SUMMER." LET'S ALL THANK CINDY FOR BRINGING THE CURRIED CAULIFLOWER AND GOAT CHEESE MARMALADE!

!

GRAM!
WELL, **HELLO**, SWEETIE! WHAT ARE YOU DOING AT THE MALL?

I WAS OVER AT KLASSIC KOMIX! I'M AN INTERN THERE!
HOW FUN!

WHAT ARE **YOU** DOING HERE?
JUST BURNING SOME CALORIES!

WE WALK AT THE MALL A FEW TIMES A WEEK! WE'RE VERY SERIOUS ABOUT OUR EXERCISE!

WE ALSO STARTED A NEW **DIET** A FEW WEEKS AGO! WE DON'T WANT TO GAIN WEIGHT IN OUR OLD AGE!

SO WE AVOID RED MEAT, FATTY FOODS, PROCESSED SUGAR...
UH... WHO'S "WE"?

YOUR **GRANDFATHER**, OF COURSE! RIGHT, VERN?

VERN?

VERN!!
A BARBECUE BACON BURGER, ONION RINGS, AND A CHOCOLATE MILKSHAKE.

COACH, I'M FILLING OUT THE LINEUP CARD. WHO'S PITCHING TODAY?
WELL, IT WAS GOING TO BE CHESTER, BUT HE'S SICK.
ACH

LORENZO'S GOT A SORE ELBOW, TEDDY AND CHAD BOTH PITCHED LAST GAME, AND KWAME IS AT THE GRAND CANYON WITH HIS FAMILY.

THAT'S OUR ENTIRE PITCHING STAFF!
I GUESS NOW WE'LL SEE HOW DEEP OUR ROSTER IS.
COACH

IN OTHER WORDS, HOW LOW CAN WE SINK?
HEY, GUYS! WATCH ME BLOW A SUNFLOWER SEED OUT MY NOSE!
CO

I GET TO PITCH?
YUP. YOU'RE THE MAN.

I KNOW YOU'VE BEEN HOPING FOR THIS, NATE, BUT IT'S JUST ANOTHER GAME! DON'T TURN IT INTO GAME 7 OF THE WORLD SERIES!

STAY LOW-KEY. TRY TO RELAX.
HEY, DUPREE OIL AND PROPANE! YOU'RE GOIN' DOWN!

...AND RESPECT YOUR OPPONENT.
OH, YOU'RE OUT OF PROPANE? NO WORRIES, I'LL BE THROWIN' GAS!
COACH

OKAY, HERE WE GO! TIME TO SHOW THESE CHUMPS MY BLAZING FASTBALL!

THIS BABY'S GOIN' RIGHT OVER THE PLATE!
WRIGHT
8

...BY ABOUT TWENTY FEET.
THAT WAS **SO** BALL ONE.
Peirce

WHAT ARE YOU **DOING**? YOU'VE WALKED THE BASES LOADED!
I HAVE A BLISTER, AND IT'S MESSING UP MY GRIP.

BUT I THINK I'VE GOT IT FIGURED OUT! I'LL JUST HOLD THE BALL A DIFFERENT WAY!
IF YOU SAY SO.

WRIGHT
8

THAT **KNUCKLED**!
STRIKE ONE!
! !

THAT WAS CRAZY! COMPLETELY BY ACCIDENT, I JUST THREW A PERFECT KNUCKLEBALL!

BUT MAYBE IT WAS A FLUKE! IF IT WAS A FLUKE, I WON'T BE ABLE TO DO IT AGAIN!

STRIKE TWO!
WRIGHT
8

Peirce

SINCE WHEN DOES YOUR PITCHER THROW A **KNUCKLEBALL**? AND HOW AM I SUPPOSED TO **HIT** IT? IT'S LIKE TRYING TO HIT A **BUTTERFLY**!

I HAVE NO IDEA WHAT I'M DOING!

WUMP!

NEITHER DOES OUR PITCHER.
HEY, **FRANCIS**! IS THIS COOL OR **WHAT**?
Peirce

THANKS TO MY INCREDIBLE KNUCKLEBALL, I'M THROWING A NO-HITTER!
YEAH, FOR THREE INNINGS!

HEY, A THREE-INNING NO-HITTER ISN'T TOO SHABBY! I DON'T SEE ANYONE ELSE DOING IT!

EXCEPT THE OTHER TEAM'S PITCHER.

HE'S NO-HITTING US, TOO.
HE IS?
WAY TO KEEP YOUR HEAD IN THE GAME.

NATE, I REALIZE YOU'VE GOT A NO-HITTER GOING, BUT THE GAME'S ONLY HALF OVER.

DON'T GET COCKY.
COCKY? **ME**?
COACH

COACH, WHEN HAVE YOU KNOWN ME TO ACT COCKY?

YOU MEAN TODAY?
I'M THE HUMBLEST GUY I KNOW! RIGHT, FELLAS? I'M **WAY** HUMBLE!
COACH

ARRGH! CAN YOU BELIEVE THIS? ON THE DAY I'M THROWING A NO-HITTER, **THEIR** PITCHER'S DOING THE **SAME THING**!

IT WOULD BE JUST MY LUCK TO BE ONE OF THOSE GUYS WHO THROWS A NO-HITTER BUT STILL **LOSES**!

NOBODY REMEMBERS WHO **LOST** A NO-HITTER! I'LL BE JUST ANOTHER HISTORICAL **ODDITY**!

IN TEN YEARS, PEOPLE MIGHT FORGET ALL **ABOUT** ME!
TO SAVE TIME, HOW ABOUT I FORGET ALL ABOUT YOU RIGHT NOW?

ALL I NEED IS ONE MORE OUT, AND I'LL HAVE MY NO-HIT GAME!

I'VE ALREADY STRUCK THIS KID OUT TWICE. HE CAN'T TOUCH MY KNUCKLEBALL!
...OR **CAN** HE?

HE'LL BE **EXPECTING** THE KNUCKLEBALL! SO IF I PUMP A **FASTBALL** IN THERE, HE'LL BE CAUGHT COMPLETELY BY SURPRISE!

I'VE GOT HIM RIGHT WHERE I WANT HIM!
WRIGHT
8
Peirce

POW!
OH, NO!
WRIGHT
8

GO FOUL.
GO FOUL!
GO FOUL!
GO FOUL!

LIFE'S NOT FAIR.
THERE GOES THE NO-HITTER.

TOUGH LOSS, NATE. BUT YOU PITCHED **GREAT**!
THANKS, DAD.

...BUT BASEBALL IS A **TEAM** GAME! MY OWN PERFORMANCE MEANS NOTHING IF THE TEAM DOESN'T WIN!

WELL, THAT'S A VERY MATURE WAY OF LOOKING AT IT, SON! I'M IMPRESSED BY YOUR ATTITUDE!

I GIVE IT TWO MINUTES.
SINCE YOU BROUGHT IT UP, THOUGH, I **WAS** PRETTY STINKIN' AWESOME OUT THERE!

HI, MISTER, DO YOU WANT TO BUY SOME RAFFLE TICKETS TO SUPPORT LITTLE LEAGUE BASEBALL?
HMM. MAYBE. MAYBE.

FIRST LET ME ASK YOU: WHO'S YOUR TEAM?

CRESSLY'S BAKERY!
NO, NO! YOUR **PRO** TEAM!

YOU MEAN, WHO DO I ROOT FOR IN MLB? THE RED SOX!
TSK. AW, THAT'S A SHAME, KID.

SEE, I'M A **YANKEES** FAN! I DON'T KNOW IF MY CONSCIENCE WILL LET ME BUY TICKETS FROM A **SOX** LOVER!

...BUT TELL YA WHAT I'LL DO: IF YOU TELL ME THAT THE YANKEES ARE THE GREATEST, I'LL BUY A WHOLE **MESS** OF TICKETS!

YOU WANT ME TO SAY I LIKE THE YANKEES?
YOU WANT THE SALE? SAY THEY'RE THE GREATEST! SIMPLE AS THAT!

THE YANKEES ARE... KOFF ...THE GREATEST.
BEAUTIFUL. THERE, WAS THAT SO HARD?

ADD THIS HOUSE TO THE HALLOWEEN EGG LIST.

CLOSE YOUR EYES AND PICTURE YOURSELF IN SOME COOL, REFRESHING PLACE.

OKAY. I'M AT THE NORTH POLE, SURROUNDED BY ICE, SNOW, AND FREEZING COLD WINDS...

IT'S HOT.
WE'VE ESTABLISHED THAT.

I'M SWEATING LIKE A PIG.
YOU'VE SAID THAT ABOUT FIFTY TIMES ALREADY.

MY SHIRT IS TOTALLY DRENCHED.
I **KNOW**! NOBODY **CARES**!

MY UNDIES ARE STARTING TO BUNCH UP.
PEIRCE

I'M LEAVING A VOICE-MAIL FOR CHANNEL 12 CHIEF METEOROLOGIST WINK SUMMERS.
beep beep boop boop beep

HELLO, WINK? HEAR THAT SOUND? KNOW WHAT IT IS?
HISSSSSSSS

IT'S AN EGG FRYING ON MY DRIVEWAY!!

WHEN WILL THIS END?
THAT'S PROBABLY WHAT WINK IS WONDER-ING ABOUT YOUR VOICEMAIL.
Peirce

FRANCIS? HEY, CAN TEDDY AND I COME OVER?... HUH? WHATTA YA MEAN, **WHY?**

BECAUSE WE'RE YOUR **BEST FRIENDS!** BECAUSE WE WANT TO HANG OUT WITH YOU! BECAUSE WE **MISS** YOU!

OKAY, AND BECAUSE YOU HAVE AIR-CONDITIONING.
TELL HIM WE'LL BRING SNACKS.
Peirce

DING
DONG

WHAM!

HI.
AHHH!
SHUT THE DOOR, FRANCIS! YOU'RE LETTING ALL THE **COOL** OUT!
Peirce

THIS AIR-CONDITIONING FEELS **AMAZING!**
EVEN THE **CARPET** IS COOL!

AHHHH! IT'S LIKE BEING IN A **POOL!**
UH... MAYBE YOU SHOULDN'T ROLL AROUND ON IT.

THE CAT'S BEEN SHEDDING A LOT LATELY.

I MIGHT THROW UP.
JUST NOT ON THE CARPET.
Peirce

WELCOME TO SWEET LICKS!
OH, MY GOSH! MR. ROSA?

YES! SORRY, DO WE KNOW ONE ANOTHER?
I'M BETH DUNPHY! I WAS A STUDENT OF YOURS! TWENTY YEARS AGO!

BETH! OF COURSE! WHAT ARE YOU UP TO THESE DAYS?
YOU'LL LOVE THIS! I'M AN ARTIST!

AND YOUR CLASS IS WHERE IT ALL STARTED! I SO ADMIRED YOUR PASSION AND DEDICATION!

I DECIDED I WANTED TO DO WHAT YOU DID, AND THAT'S JUST WHAT I'VE DONE!
WELL, THAT'S AWFULLY NICE TO HEAR!

SO... YOU TEACH IN A MIDDLE SCHOOL?
NO, AT YALE.

I'M ON SABBATICAL AT THE MOMENT TO FOCUS ON MY UPCOMING RETROSPECTIVE AT THE MUSEUM OF MODERN ART, BUT NEXT YEAR I'LL BE BACK IN NEW HAVEN!

I FEEL AN ICE CREAM HEADACHE COMING ON.
AND HOW ARE YOU?

AHH! HOW GREAT IS THIS?

THE SUN IS OUT... THE AIR IS FRESH... AND WHAT AM I DOING?

EARNING FORTY BUCKS FOR UMPING A LITTLE LEAGUE BALLGAME!

YUP! CAN'T BEAT IT!

I'D DO THIS FOR FREE!

OW!
?

OW! OW! OW! OW! OW!

FOOT CRAMP! FOOT CRAMP! FOOT CRAMP!
THEY'RE NOT PAYING ME ENOUGH.

THERE'S SOMETHING I HAVE TO TELL SOMEONE.
SO?

SO, IT'S SOMETHING HE WON'T BE HAPPY ABOUT! SOMETHING THAT MIGHT HURT HIS FEELINGS!
WELL, JUST DON'T SUGAR-COAT IT, DUDE.

THE BEST WAY TO HANDLE SITUATIONS LIKE THAT IS TO BE HONEST.
YOU'RE RIGHT!

SPITSY, WE NEED TO TALK.
Peirce

SPITSY, THIS WON'T BE EASY TO HEAR, BUT I'M JUST GONNA GO AHEAD AND SAY IT.

YOU HAVE BAD BREATH.

WURF?

OWOOOOOo
HE'S VERY SENSITIVE.
peirce

SORRY I HURT YOUR FEELINGS, SPITSY... BUT ISN'T IT BETTER TO **KNOW** YOU HAVE BAD BREATH?

NOW WE CAN FOCUS ON MAKING IT **BETTER!** OKAY? C'MON, BUDDY! DON'T BE SAD!

SIIIGH...

BEFORE WE GO ANY FURTHER, I NEED TO TAKE A BRIEF MENTAL HEALTH BREAK.
Peirce

IF WE WANT TO FIX YOUR HALITOSIS PROBLEM, SPITSY, WE HAVE TO FIGURE OUT WHAT'S GIVING YOU BAD BREATH IN THE **FIRST** PLACE!

I'LL USE MY SUPER SENSE OF SMELL TO IDENTIFY EVERYTHING YOU'VE EATEN IN THE LAST 24 HOURS!

SNIFF! KIBBLE, SEAWEED, TERIYAKI SAUCE, MAYONNAISE, SOUR MILK, BROCCOLI, ROAD KILL, ROTTEN EGGS, GOAT CHEESE, AND...

TELL ME I'M NOT SMELLING CAT POOP.
MEOW!
Peirce

TO FIX YOUR BAD BREATH, SPITSY, WE NEED TO REPLACE THE NASTY STUFF YOU **USUALLY** EAT WITH **GOOD**-SMELLING FOOD!

AND NOTHING SMELLS BETTER THAN A BAG OF **CHEEZ DOODLES**! WOO-HOO!
SNIFF SNIFF

PYOO!

I DON'T EVEN KNOW WHO YOU ARE ANYMORE.
MUNCH MUNCH MUNCH
Peirce

DID YOU SOLVE SPITSY'S HALITOSIS PROBLEM?
NO. HIS BREATH IS STILL BRUTAL.

I THINK I MADE HIM FEEL BAD BY POINTING IT OUT TO HIM... BUT WHAT WAS I **SUP-POSED** TO DO?

I MEAN, IF **I** HAD BAD BREATH, I'D WANT A FRIEND TO TELL **ME**.
YEAH.

ALTOID?
OOH! SURE!
Peirce

LIQUID
REFRESHMENT
$ 1.00

WHAT ARE YOU SELLING?
READ THE SIGN, GINA! LIQUID REFRESHMENT!

WHAT KIND OF LIQUID REFRESH-MENT?
PAY ME A BUCK AND FIND OUT!

YOU THINK I'M A FOOL? THIS IS ONE OF YOUR TRICKS!

AS SOON AS I GIVE YOU A DOLLAR, YOU'LL SPRAY ME WITH A HOSE!
NO, I WON'T!

SWEAR IT.
I SWEAR I WON'T SPRAY YOU WITH A HOSE.

OKAY, THEN. HERE.
LIQUID REFRESH-MENT, COMIN' UP!

YANK!

SPLOOSH!

I HATE YOU SO MUCH.
FOR ANOTHER DOLLAR, YOU CAN RENT A TOWEL!
LIQUID
REFRESHMENT
$ 1.00
peirce

HEY, **HEY**! WANT TO GO SHOPPING FOR SCHOOL SUPPLIES?
WITH **YOU**? NO.

OH, COME **ON**! IT'LL BE **FUN**!
NO, IT **WON'T**! IT'LL BE **EMBARRASSING**!

WHAT? WHEN HAVE I EVER EMBARRASSED YOU DURING BACK-TO-SCHOOL SHOPPING?
LAST YEAR!

YOU **CRIED** IN THE 3-RING BINDER AISLE!
TEARS OF **JOY**!

HI, WELCOME TO OFFICE HUB.
HI.

HI, WELCOME TO OFFICE HUB.
H'LO.

FRANCIS!
WHAT'S UP, WENDELL?

I COME HERE A LOT TO BROWSE!
THAT'S DEEPLY DISTURBING.

AH! ISN'T THIS INVIGORATING?
INVIGORATING? IT'S AN OFFICE SUPPLIES STORE!

EXACTLY! AND EACH ITEM ON THESE SHELVES HOLDS THE PROMISE OF EXCITING NEW ACCOMPLISHMENTS!

LIKE THIS BOX OF PENCILS! THINK OF WHAT A PERSON COULD DO WITH THESE PENCILS!
HMM... YEAH, THEY **DO** HAVE POTENTIAL.

WHAP!
peirce

LOOK AT THIS! THEY'RE CHARGING EIGHT DOLLARS FOR THIS NOTE-BOOK! EIGHT DOLLARS!
SO?

IT'S AN INFERIOR PRODUCT! THE STORAGE POCKETS AREN'T REINFORCED! THE TABS AREN'T COLOR-CODED!

DO THEY THINK I'M AN **IDIOT**? AFTER ALL THE SUPPLIES I'VE BOUGHT HERE, **THIS** IS THE THANKS I GET?

I'M BITTERLY DISAPPOINTED IN YOU.
SO IS MY MOTHER. SHE WANTED ME TO BE A PEDIATRICIAN.

WHERE CAN I FIND RUBBER BANDS?
AISLE THREE, ON THE LEFT.

WHAT'S THE DIFFERENCE BETWEEN THESE TWO BINDERS?
UM...THAT ONE'S GOT ONE EXTRA POCKET.

WHY IS RHYTHMIC GYMNASTICS AN OLYMPIC SPORT WHEN BASEBALL **ISN'T**? ANSWER **THAT** ONE!

THAT BUTTON YOU'RE WEARING SAYS "ASK ME ANYTHING."
I HATE THIS JOB.
Peirce

THESE ARE ALL THE SAME.
AREN'T THEY **SUPPOSED** TO BE THE SAME?
DS

SOME PEOPLE MIGHT FEEL THAT WAY, BUT **I**, FOR ONE, PREFER A LITTLE **VARIETY**!
F

EXCUSE ME, I'M LOOKING FOR THESE, BUT WITH A BIT MORE ATTITUDE. A BIT MORE SASS.
F

YOU WANT SASSY INDEX CARDS?
INDEED I DO.
OH, BROTHER.
F
Peirce

WHAT HAVE YOU GOT THERE, SPITSY?

HEY, ISN'T THAT MIRANDA'S DOLL?

YOU'D BETTER GIVE IT BACK TO HER, SPITSY. SHE'LL BE MAD.

COME ON, GIVE IT HERE.
GRRRRR!

OKAY, FINE! YOU TOOK IT, SO IT'S YOU SHE'LL COME LOOKING FOR!

GIVE ME BACK MY DOLLY, OR I'LL TURN YOU INTO A RUG.

IN THE NEIGHBORHOOD FOOD CHAIN, A DOG IS SEVERAL STEPS BELOW A QUEEN BEE.
Peirce

Look for these books!

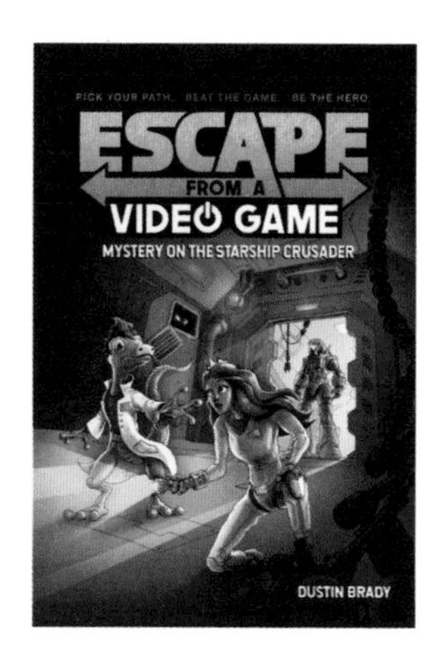

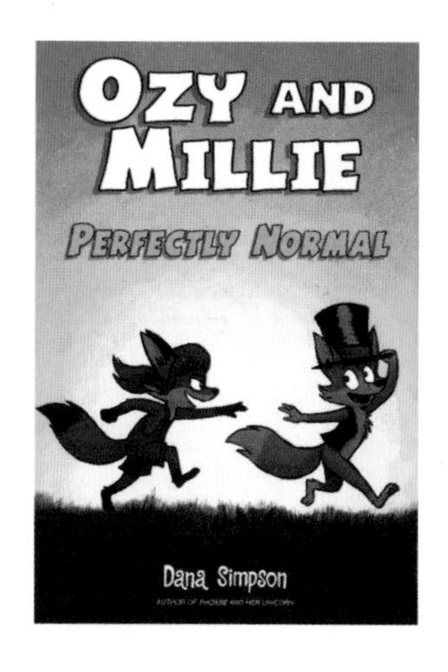

Big Nate is distributed internationally by Andrews McMeel Syndication.

Andrews McMeel Publishing
a division of Andrews McMeel Universal
1130 Walnut Street, Kansas City, Missouri 64106

www.andrewsmcmeel.com

21 22 23 24 25 SDB 10 9 8 7 6 5 4 3 2 1

ISBN: 978-1-5248-6856-7

Library of Congress Control Number: 2021932765

Made by:
King Yip (Dongguan) Printing & Packaging Factory Ltd.
Address and location of manufacturer:
Daning Administrative District, Humen Town
Dongguan Guangdong, China 523930
1st Printing—5/24/21

These strips appeared in newspapers from
February 26, 2017, through September 2, 2017.

Big Nate can be viewed on the Internet at
www.gocomics.com/big_nate.